Indiana
PACERS

BY JIM GIGLIOTTI

Published by The Child's World®
1980 Lookout Drive • Mankato, MN 56003-1705
800-599-READ • www.childsworld.com

Cover: © Joe Robbins.
Interior Photographs ©: AP Images: John Lent 9; Michael Conroy 17; Ben
Margot 18. Imagn/USA Today Sports: Jayne Kamin-Oncea 10. Newscom:
John J. Kim/TNS 6; Brian Spurlock 25, 26; Icon SMI 22; Harry Walker/
KRT 29. Joe Robbins: 5, 13, 21, 26 (3).

ISBN 9781503824539
LCCN 2018964281

Printed in the United States of America
PA02416

ABOUT THE AUTHOR

Jim Gigliotti has worked for the University of Southern California's athletic department, the Los Angeles Dodgers, and the National Football League. He is now an author who has written more than 100 books, mostly for young readers, on a variety of topics.

TABLE OF CONTENTS

GO, PACERS!

Sports fans in Indiana love basketball. They especially love the Pacers. The fans support the team through good times and not-so-good times. The good times include three titles in the American Basketball Association (ABA). That was the league the Pacers started in. The Pacers are still looking for their first NBA title. When it comes, their fans will be ready to celebrate.

Indiana's superstar is Victor Oladipo.
A great scorer, he also plays solid defense.

Myles Turner is the youngest regular starter for the Pacers. He has improved every season.

WHO ARE THE PACERS?

The Pacers play in the NBA Central Division. That division is part of the Eastern Conference. The other teams in the Central Division are the Chicago Bulls, the Cleveland Cavaliers, the Detroit Pistons, and the Milwaukee Bucks. The Pacers have won the Central Division six times. They made it to the NBA Finals in 2000.

WHERE THEY CAME FROM

The Pacers began in the ABA in 1968. They made the ABA **playoffs** nine years in a row. They reached the Finals five times. The Pacers joined the NBA in 1977. The team got its name from auto racing. A "pace" car helps start some car races. The Indianapolis 500 is held in Indiana each year. It is one of the most famous car races in the world.

Check out the short shorts and striped basketball in this ABA action photo from 1967.

9

Bojan Bogdanovic rises to shoot against the Western Conference's Lakers.

The Pacers play 82 games each season. They play 41 games at home and 41 on the road. They play four games against each of the other Central Division teams. They play 36 games against other Eastern Conference teams. They play each of the teams in the Western Conference twice. Each June, the winners of the Western and Eastern Conferences play each other in the NBA Finals.

The Pacers have some of the best fans in the NBA. The team is very popular. It plays in Indianapolis, the capital city of Indiana. Pacers fans pack the Bankers Life Fieldhouse. A **mascot** named Boomer entertains the fans. The arena is modern, but it has an old-fashioned look. That is on purpose. Basketball has a long history in Indiana.

Boomer the mascot makes regular visits to the Pacers' home court. Riding a bike or doing slam dunks, he helps fans cheer.

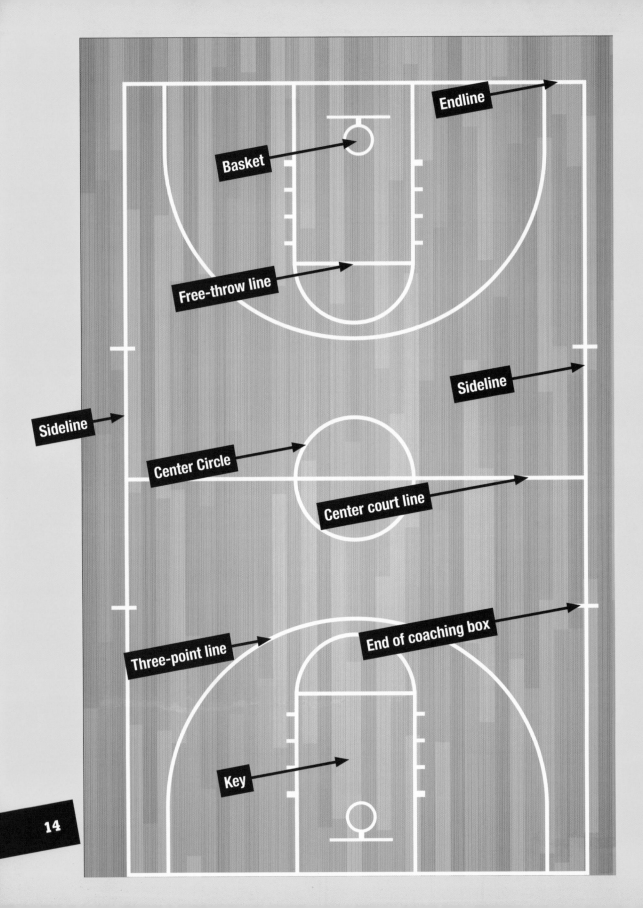

THE BASKETBALL COURT

An NBA court is 94 feet long and 50 feet wide (28.6 m by 15.24 m). Nearly all the courts are made from hard maple wood. Rubber mats under the wood help make the floor springy. Each team paints the court with its **logo** and colors. Lines on the court show the players where to take shots. The diagram on the left shows the important parts of the NBA court.

Bankers Life Fieldhouse twice has been named the top arena in the NBA by a famous sports business website.

R eggie Miller could score points in a hurry. He poured in 25 points in the fourth quarter of a 1994 playoff game. The Pacers beat the Knicks. Miller led another win over the Knicks in the next year's playoffs. He scored eight points in nine seconds late in the game. The Pacers won the Eastern Conference in 2000 and played in the NBA Finals. In 2004, they won a team-record 61 games.

Indiana's Austin Croshere slams home two points during the 2000 NBA Finals against the Lakers.

Indiana got tired of seeing Klay Thompson signal another three. In a 2017 game, the Warriors forward scored 60 points against Indiana.

The Pacers hit a rough patch after joining the NBA. They missed the playoffs four years in a row. The team won fewer than 30 games five times in the 1980s. The 1983 team had only 20 wins. Early in the 2017 season, Klay Thompson scored 60 points for the Golden State Warriors against the Pacers. He played only 29 minutes in that 48-minute game. The Warriors won by 36 points.

ALL THE RIGHT MOVES

Indiana's Reggie Miller was a great three-point shooter. He led the league in three-pointers made in both 1993 and 1997. He launched high rainbow shots. They often swished through the basket. Miller made way more three-pointers than anyone else in team history. Today Victor Oladipo is the Pacers top three-point shooter.

Want to learn some NBA slang? Three-point shots are also called "treys." A great assist is called a "dime."

Victor Oladipo launches another three-point shot. The sharpshooter has made this long-range shot his favorite.

Reggie Miller spent his entire 18-year Hall of Fame career shooting hoops for Indiana.

Mel Daniels was a star in the ABA. He is in the **Hall of Fame**. The Pacers made the playoffs 10 times with Rik Smits at center. Reggie Miller played 18 years with the Pacers. He was one of the top shooters in NBA history. Jermaine O'Neal was an all-star six years in a row in the 2000s. Paul George was an all-star four times in the 2010s.

Victor Oladipo is a high-scoring **guard**. Domantas Sabonis is a young **center**. He does it all. He scores, rebounds, and passes the ball well. Oladipo and Sabonis joined the Pacers in 2018. They came to the team in a big trade. Then Doug McDermott joined the team in 2019. So did veteran Tyreke Evans. This group of young players gives Pacers fans high hopes.

Domantas Sabonis learned his hoops at home. His father Arvydas played in the NBA.

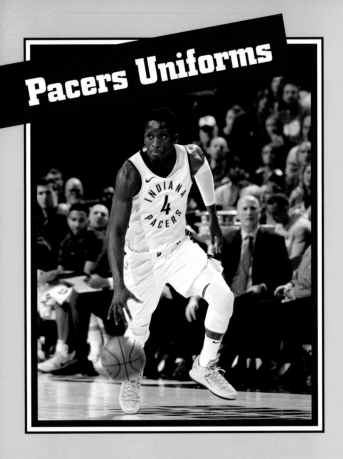

WHAT THEY WEAR

NBA players wear a **tank top** jersey. Players wear team shorts. Each player can choose his own sneakers. Some players also wear knee pads or wrist guards.

Each NBA team has more than one jersey style. The pictures at left show some of the Pacers' jerseys.

The NBA basketball is 29.5 inches (75 cm) around. It is covered with leather. The leather has small bumps called pebbles.

The pebbles on a basketball help players grip it.

Here are some of the all-time career records for the Indiana Pacers. These stats are complete through all of the 2018–19 NBA regular season.

GAMES

Reggie Miller	1,389
Rik Smits	867

POINTS PER GAME

Victor Oladipo	21.7
George McGinnis	19.6

STEALS PER GAME

Don Buse	2.55
Micheal Williams	2.52

REBOUNDS PER GAME

Mel Daniels	16.0
George McGinnis	10.7

THREE-POINT FIELD GOALS

Reggie Miller	2,560
Danny Granger	964

FREE-THROW PCT.

Chris Mullin	.912
John Long	.902

MARK JACKSON

ASSISTS PER GAME

Mark Jackson	8.1
Pooh Richardson	7.3

GLOSSARY

center *(SEN-ter)* a basketball position that plays near the basket

guard *(GARD)* a player in basketball who usually dribbles and makes passes

Hall of Fame *(HALL UV FAYM)* a building in Springfield, Massachusetts, that honors basketball heroes

logo *(LOW-go)* a team or company's symbol

mascot *(MASS-kot)* a costumed character who helps fans cheer

playoffs *(PLAY-offs)* games played between top teams to determine who moves ahead

tank top *(TANK TOP)* a style of shirt that has straps over the shoulders and no sleeves

FIND OUT MORE

IN THE LIBRARY

Big Book of Who: Basketball (Sports Illustrated Kids Big Books). New York, NY: Sports Illustrated Kids, 2015.

Schaller, Bob with Coach Dave Harnish. *The Everything Kids' Basketball Book (3rd Edition).* Avon, MA: Adams Media, 2017.

Walters, John. *Top Ten Basketball Superstars (Top Ten in Sports).* Mankato, MN: The Child's World, 2018.

ON THE WEB

Visit our website for links about the Indiana Pacers:

childsworld.com/links

Note to Parents, Teachers, and Librarians: We routinely verify our Web links to make sure they are safe and active sites. So encourage your readers to check them out!

INDEX